Pinky and Rex
Go To Camp

JAMES HOWE is the author of numerous popular books for children, including *The Fright Before Christmas* and *Scared Silly,* and other books about Bunnicula, the vampire rabbit, and his friends, Harold, Chester, and Howie.

The Pinky and Rex books were inspired in part by a child's question about the author's favorite color (he was wearing a pink shirt that day) and by his friendship when he was seven with a girl very much like Rex.

Mr. Howe lives in Hastings-on-Hudson, New York, with his wife, Betsy Imershein, and their daughter, Zoe.

MELISSA SWEET has studied art at the Kansas City Art Institute and currently works as a greeting card illustrator and maker of one-of-a-kind, handmade collector's books. With the Pinky and Rex series, she now enters the world of children's book illustration. Ms. Sweet lives in Boston, Massachusetts, with her husband.

Pinky and Rex Go To Camp

JAMES HOWE
Illustrated by Melissa Sweet

AN AVON CAMELOT BOOK

AVON BOOKS
A division of
The Hearst Corporation
1350 Avenue of the Americas
New York, New York 10019

Text copyright © 1992 by James Howe
Illustrations copyright © 1992 by Melissa Sweet
Published by arrangement with Atheneum Publishers, an imprint of Macmillan Publishing
Company
Library of Congress Catalog Card Number: 91-16123
ISBN: 0-380-72082-5
RL: 2.3

First Avon Camelot Printing: May 1993

CAMELOT TRADEMARK REG. U.S. PAT. OFF. AND IN OTHER COUNTRIES, MARCA REGISTRADA,
HECHO EN U.S.A.

Printed in the U.S.A.

ARC   10   9   8   7   6   5   4   3   2   1

To my brother, Doug

—J. H.

To Alison

—M. S.

Contents

Chapter 1
Camp Wackatootchee

"Pinky! Pinky!"

Rex knocked loudly on Pinky's front door. "I got my letter!" she cried. "Did you get yours?"

Pinky came to the door and opened it slowly. "Yes," he said, letting his friend in. "What's so exciting about it?"

"What's so exciting about it? It tells us all the stuff we need to bring with us to Camp Wackatootchee. And look," said Rex, pointing to one of the papers in her hands, "here's the camp song. My dad's been teaching me the melody."

2

Before he could stop her, Rex burst out singing at the top of her lungs:

"Boom, boom, boom! Hear the
    tom-tom's beat,
Camp Wackatootchee, you're so neat!
Blue and orange, orange and blue,
Camp Wackatootchee, we love you!

"Around the tepee we gather nightly,
To sing camp songs and do what's rightly.
We all will miss you when we go home,
But in our hearts we'll never roam."

Rex beamed. "Isn't that the greatest song?" she asked.

"Uh-huh," said Pinky flatly, "the greatest. Um, Rex, I have to clean up my room now." And he turned and headed up the stairs.

Rex followed after him. "What's the matter, Pinky?" she said. "I thought you *wanted* to go to sleep-away camp."

"I do," said Pinky. He led Rex into his room, which wasn't messy at all. "Who said I didn't?"

"Well, you're acting kind of funny."

"I just don't feel so good," said Pinky. "Amanda made muffins for breakfast and I think she must have left something out."

"I heard that!"

Pinky's little sister, Amanda, stood scowling at the door. "I didn't leave anything out of those muffins and you know it, Pinky. They were scrumptious. Mom even said so."

"Moms have to say things like
that," said Pinky. He flopped down
on his bed.

"Hmph!" said Amanda, crossing
her arms. She was about to leave the
room when she turned back and said

to Rex, "I heard you singing that dumb song. I'll tell you one thing. I'm glad *I'm* not going away to camp. Poison ivy, snakes, cougars—forget it. And I'll tell you one other thing: Those camp counselors may look like real people, but at night they turn into monsters and they'll eat you up while you're sleeping."

With her nose in the air, Amanda flounced out of the room.

"Don't listen to her," Rex said.

But it was too late. Pinky already had.

Chapter 2
"Dear Arnie"

That night after dinner, Pinky wrote a letter to Arnie. Arnie was someone who gave people advice about their problems. The letters, and Arnie's answers, appeared in the newspaper in a column called "Dear Arnie."

That is what Pinky wrote first: "Dear Arnie."

Then he stopped and chewed on his pencil for a minute while he thought of what to write next. When he had figured it out, he wrote:

My mom and dad are making me go away to camp and this is not something I want to do. It all started because my best friend is going and so my mom and dad got this idea that I wanted to go too, but I don't (like I said). Please answer my letter soon because camp starts in three weeks and if I have to go I will probably run away, which I don't want to do either because the whole thing is I don't want to go anywhere. I want to stay home where I belong.

Sincerely,

Pinky stopped writing. He knew
that people who wrote letters to
Arnie always made up names for
themselves. He wasn't sure why; it
was probably because they didn't
want their friends making fun of
them. He thought for a long time,
then wrote:

                    Miserable Max
    P.S. Miserable Max is not my real
    name.

Pinky read the letter over carefully. It was a good letter, he thought, and he was proud of the fact that he hadn't had to look up the spelling of any of the words, not even *miserable*. Then he carefully copied Arnie's address from the newspaper, put the letter into an envelope, and put the envelope under his pillow. He would mail it first thing the next morning.

Chapter 3
Practice

Every day Pinky checked the newspaper for Arnie's answer to his letter. Two weeks went by. Arnie answered a man whose wife snored so loudly he couldn't sleep. He answered a woman who didn't know how to tell her husband that his cooking was making her sick. He answered a girl whose parents wouldn't let her get her ears pierced.

But he didn't answer Pinky. Pinky
began to worry that Arnie had never
received his letter.

All the while, Rex was getting
more and more excited about camp.

"Come on," she said to Pinky
one sunny morning, "it's a perfect

day for practicing your fastball." She
kept slamming a ball into the
catcher's mitt she'd gotten for her
last birthday.

"What fastball?" Pinky muttered.
"Anyway, I don't want to practice,
Rex. Let's ride our bikes."

"Aw, Pinky," Rex said, "we can ride our bikes anytime. We need to get in shape for camp. Just think, two whole weeks of softball and volleyball and tennis and swimming and boating and—"

"Okay, okay," said Pinky. The more Rex talked, the more Pinky's stomach began to hurt.

"My dad's been practicing with me every night when he comes home from work," Rex said as they ran across the yard. "I'll show you some of the neat stuff he taught me."

She tossed Pinky her mitt. "First, you catch and I'll throw," she said. "Ready?"

"Ready as I'll ever be," said Pinky.

He watched as Rex squinted her eyes, wound up her pitching arm, and sent the ball flying so fast he could hardly see where it was going. He scrambled to catch it but missed by a few feet and tumbled into a bush.

"You weren't trying!" Rex shouted as she ran to retrieve the ball.

"Was too!" Pinky shouted back. He could feel his cheeks growing hot.

Pinky missed the next ball. And the next. And the next. Finally he threw the mitt on the ground and said, "Forget it, Rex. I'm no good."

"You just need practice," said Rex. "My dad says practice makes—"

But Pinky didn't wait to find out what Rex's dad said. He was already most of the way home.

Chapter 4
Orange and Blue

The next day Pinky's mother took him shopping for camp clothes. Amanda came along.

"I don't know why Mom's wasting money on new clothes when you're only going to end up being eaten by camp counselors," Amanda whispered in Pinky's ear after Pinky

had tried on about a million shirts
and pairs of shorts. "Or who knows,
maybe you'll fall in the lake and the
piranha fish will get you."

"Stop it, Amanda," said Pinky.

He looked up at the pile of
clothes on the counter. Everything
was orange or blue. These were not
his favorite colors.

"Why do I have to wear those?"
he grumbled.

"Because everyone is asked to
wear Camp Wackatootchee colors,"
his mother told him. "Besides, Pinky,
it will be a nice change from what
you usually wear. Everyone needs a
change now and then."

"I don't," Pinky said, but so
softly no one heard.

After they had bought
everything Pinky needed for camp,
his mother suggested that they stop
for ice cream.

As she dug into her hot fudge
sundae, Amanda licked her lips and
said cheerfully, "You know, Pinky,
you're not going to be able to take
your stuffed animals to camp with
you." This thought hadn't occurred

to Pinky before. He looked at
Amanda with wide eyes. "So guess
what?" she went on. "I'm going to
keep all of them in my room."

"No way!" Pinky said. He said it
so loudly the people at the next table
looked over to see what was wrong.

"Well, you're not going to be
here," Amanda said. "So there's
nothing you can do about it."

"Mom!" Pinky fairly shouted.

"Ssh," said Pinky's mother. Then turning to Amanda, she said, "Pinky's animals will stay in his room where they belong."

"But—"

"End of discussion, Amanda. I don't want Pinky to have to worry about his animals while he's gone."

"But, Mom," said Pinky, "can't I even take Pretzel?" Pretzel was a pig, and Pinky's favorite.

"Of course you can."

Pinky smiled as Amanda stuck out her tongue at him. But his smile quickly faded. He wondered what else he might have to worry about while he was away. Two whole weeks. Amanda could cause a lot of trouble in two whole weeks. He thought about getting a lock for his room, but he knew his parents wouldn't let him.

Suddenly he wasn't hungry anymore.

"If you aren't going to finish that," Amanda said, eyeing his half-eaten dish of ice cream, "I will."

Chapter 5
Arnie's Answer

It was the day before camp was to begin. Pinky had stayed in his bedroom with the door closed all morning. He had told his mother he was going to pack, but instead he'd spent the whole time reading comics and thinking about running away from home.

Amanda was at day camp, so the house was very quiet.

All at once, there was a knock on his door.

"Pinky?" his mother called softly. "May I come in?"

Pinky jumped up. Quickly he threw his suitcase on the bed and tossed some clothes into it. "Sure," he said.

The door opened. Pinky's mother entered, with a newspaper tucked under her arm. "Almost finished packing?" she asked.

"Sort of," said Pinky.

His mother smiled when she saw the jumble of clothes on the bed. "You pack the way your father does," she said. Then she unfolded the newspaper. "May we talk for a minute, Pinky?"

Pinky's mother moved the suitcase and sat down on the bed. "There's something I'd like you to see," she said, patting the bed. Pinky sat down next to her. He saw at once that the newspaper was open to "Dear Arnie." "I think you'll find that first letter interesting," she said.

Pinky could hardly believe it.
There at last was his letter to Arnie.
He didn't bother reading it; it was all
there, every word. There too was
Arnie's answer.

Dear Miserable Max,

If this is your first time staying away from home, I can understand why you don't want to go. After all, it can be very scary to leave everything you know and stay someplace brand new. But I would guess your parents know you well enough that they feel you'll do just fine. Besides, camp is a great growing experience. Believe it or not, you'll feel a lot older by the time you come home.

Pinky smirked. What did he care about feeling a lot older? Then he read:

P.S. Have you told your parents how you feel?

Pinky didn't know what to say. Luckily, his mother spoke first.

"You know, Pinky, you never told us you didn't want to go to camp."

"What do you mean?" Pinky asked. Then pretending to laugh, he

said, "Oh, I get it, you think *I* wrote this letter. But Mom, my name isn't Max. And, anyway—"

"It doesn't matter if you wrote the letter or not. What matters is what you want. Do you *want* to go to Camp Wackatootchee, Pinky? Be honest."

Pinky sat for a long time. Being honest was going to be hard.

Finally he said, "No, I really don't."

His mother nodded her head and thought for a minute. What she said next surprised Pinky. "Well then, you don't have to go. We'll discuss it with your father after dinner tonight, but I just want you to know right now that we're not going to force you to do this. Okay, Pinky?"

Pinky was so relieved he almost felt like crying. "Okay," he said. And he gave his mother a big hug.

Chapter 6
Telling Rex

It was decided. Pinky was not going to Camp Wackatootchee. His father didn't say anything about the money. His mother never mentioned the clothes she'd bought for him. Only Amanda said something about how he was probably afraid of being eaten by camp counselors and he was just a big coward.

After he'd talked with his
parents, Pinky went across the street
to break the news to Rex. All the way
over, he practiced what he would say.

But when Rex saw him coming,
she didn't give him a chance to say
anything.

"Follow me," she said, running
to her backyard. The two friends sat
side by side on the swings.

"I have something to tell you,"
Rex told Pinky.

Pinky looked at her, wondering what she was about to say.

"I'm scared about going to camp," Rex said.

"Really?" Pinky stopped swinging. "I thought you wanted to go."

"I do," said Rex. "But I'm still scared. I can't tell my dad, because he's so excited about my going to the same camp he used to go to. And I can't tell my mom because she'd tell my dad. But I knew I could tell you, Pinky, because we're best friends. Are you scared too?"

"Well, yes—"

"Good," Rex said. Then she laughed. "I don't mean it's good you're scared. But I'm glad I'm not the only one. You know, Pinky, if you

weren't going to camp with me, I'd
be really, really scared instead of just
a little scared."

Pinky wasn't sure what to say.

"Are you all packed?" Rex
asked. "I am."

"No," said Pinky.

"Then you'd better hurry up,"
Rex said. "The camp bus is picking us
up first thing in the morning."

Pinky knew this was the time to
tell Rex he wasn't going. But he
didn't tell her that. Instead, he said,
"Okay. I'll see you in the morning."

And he ran home to pack.

Chapter 7
"Dear Amanda"

"Dear Amanda," Pinky wrote
after his first week at camp,

I am having a great time here at
Camp Wackatootchee. I learned
how to shoot a bow and arrow and
I can swim underwater without
nose plugs. My counselor's name
is Bill. He said to tell you that
counselors do not like to eat

campers. But they do like little sisters with ketchup. Rex said to tell you hi. Even though the boys' camp is on one side of the lake and the girls' camp is on the other side, Rex and I see each other every day at Tepee Time. Well, I have to go now. I hope you will get to go to camp someday, Amanda. Maybe it will help you grow up.

(signed) Your brother,
Pinky

"Dear Pinky," Amanda wrote back. "Watch out for the alligators."